THE EXERCISE

a novella by
Mark West

The Exercise

Published by PenMan Press

Originally published as part of *Darker Battlefields*, edited by Adrian Chamberlin, published by theEXAGGERATEDpress in 2016.

This revised version published by PenMan Press 2021

text and cover design © Mark West 2021

for two very good men:
My Dad, Graham West, for his love, support and
encouragement
and
my Grampy, Ray West, who bravely served

The Exercise

Somewhere in the Fens, East Anglia, August, 1943

One

The moon hung, half-full and high, in an almost
cloudless sky. Other than the soft pale blue of its
light, the night was very dark, streetlights
extinguished due to the blackouts.

Robin Wickes didn't worry about the darkness,
he knew these roads like the back of his hand and
made his way steadily along the verge. He kept
close to the hedge, not wanting to be spotted by any
of the guards, determined in the mission he'd been
planning for a while now. Well, a couple of weeks
at least.

The lane was boxed in with Ash trees and just
behind those to his left was the river Thurne. The
lane ended at Sinclair House and he could already
make out the dark bulk of its perimeter stone wall, at
least ten feet high, the front elevation partly masked
by tall Poplars.

Like everyone else in the village, he and his
friends assumed the house was being used to keep
prisoners of war. None of them really knew -
though most of them had kept up with the gossip
their mothers happily exchanged over the garden
fences - but almost everyone had heard the screams
at one time or another and there was no other reason
for all the armed soldiers standing guard.

What Robin did know was that they kept
chickens and rabbits and had a big orchard. And in
these times of rationing and the black market, that
was enough to get him out in the dark.

He'd watched the house for a fortnight. Guards
patrolled inside the walls, all of them armed, but
none came through the gate. The perimeter wall was

solid and he'd tried climbing a section at the back of the house but failed. He daren't bring the gang because he was afraid one of them would blab, which was a shame because he could have stood on Ginger Grubshaw's shoulders and seen over the wall easily. Then he found the old wooden door. Apparently forgotten, it was obscured by the trunk of a tree, ivy growing from it and linking to the wall but a resourceful schoolboy, with time on his hands, could easily burrow through. Which was exactly what Robin had done. It had taken him the best part of a week, working in small bursts to avoid the guards, but he'd got through the unlocked door and that's when he'd discovered the chickens, rabbits and orchard. A veritable treasure chest.

Tonight he made his way straight there. He shrugged off his gasmask box and hid it by the tree, forced his way through the ivy and pushed the rough door open enough to slip through. The wood was rotting and as he brushed by it more stuck to his cardigan than had yesterday, when he'd found a couple of long splinters buried in the wool.

He'd never been in Sinclair House but it looked very posh from his vantage point, hidden behind a bush. It was old fashioned, stone-built, with fancy gargoyles on the roof and lots of windows, all X'd against bombing raids. There were even some windows in the attic! The wide expanse of lawn he could see wasn't so posh though, it needed mowing. To his left, a gravel drive led from the gate to the front door, which you had to go up steps to. He'd seen some lorries drive up, dropping off and picking up whatever they were dropping off and picking up. To his right was where the grounds really opened up

- about a hundred yards away was the large chicken run and beyond that were four Nissen huts, just inside the tree-line of the orchard that ran to the back of the property.

Prisoners, people said. Robin had never seen a German in real life, though he was sure he'd know one because they were snivelling cowards who shot you in the back, but the area was prepared for them and their attack, with several pill-boxes between here and the coast. He and his gang sometimes played around them, especially when the younger Home Guard were on, because they remembered being children. The older Home Guard were more serious and would quite happily chase off young boys, shouting threats and gesturing with rusty old bayonets strapped to their rifles.

Movement caught his eye and he ducked behind the bush as a lone soldier came from the drive, carrying a Sten gun. He stopped when he reached the lawn, slung the gun over his shoulder and took a crumpled pack of smokes from his breast pocket. Something made him twist around quickly and Robin watched him look this way and that, turning slowly, until he was seemingly satisfied enough to light his cigarette. The harsh, sweet smell drifted over to Robin who inhaled hopefully. A chicken squawked.

The soldier smoked his cigarette where he stood, finally stamping it out on the grass and throwing the tiny butt into the bush. He coughed, took one last look around then walked back to the drive and out of sight.

Robin took that as his cue and, with his back to the wall, edged along until he'd cleared the bush.

The chicken coop was about fifty yards away and he could hear them, clucking at one another quietly. There were some shapes on the grass he couldn't quite make out properly but thought they looked like eggs.

Robin slipped his knapsack off and, crouching low, duck-walked to the coop. He was halfway there when he heard someone shout - he couldn't make out what they said, but it didn't sound happy. He looked up towards the Nissen huts. People seemed to be moving about. There was another shout, louder this time and unmistakably angry. Running footsteps sounded on the gravel behind him. He was caught in the middle.

"Bollocks," he said, feeling a terrible cold sweat on his forehead.

More footsteps on the gravel. It wouldn't be long until they reached the lawn and saw him. There was an angry shout from the Nissen huts and something else, a sound like a crowd at a football match. Robin pushed away from the coop and its potential eggs, aiming for the bush.

"Stop!" someone yelled and he froze, his heart thudding in his chest and wrists. What would he say, what could he say? This was the cane, for sure and probably a proper leathering from Dad too.

"I said stop!" yelled the same voice. Robin hadn't moved, which meant he hadn't been seen so he quickly pushed himself back.

A single shot was fired, which filled the night with sound and made the silence that followed it even noisier. Nobody moved on the gravel but he could hear someone running, the heavy thud of their step indicating they were moving fast. A shape came towards him from the orchard, arms flailing as if trying to keep balance.

"I said stop!" yelled the voice, "or I'll fire."

The runner kept moving and the guns responded. There were several single shots, probably from Lee Enfield number fours. Robin knew his guns, he knew what they sounded like and prided himself on his knowledge.

The Sten guns rattled into life. Several 9mm bullets thudded into the wall behind Robin, showering him with stone dust. He flinched, covered his face.

The runner bumped his leg against the side of the chicken run, the limb flicking out at an odd angle and cartwheeling the man across the lawn. More bullets hit the lawn, ripping holes into the grass. Robin was three feet away from the bush and, it seemed, still in the firing line.

A searchlight burst into life from the roof, its beam quickly directed onto the lawn. Robin closed his eyes against the glare but the imprint of the man running towards him, his left leg moving at an impossible angle, stayed with him. There were more shouts, more gunshots, then someone yelled "There's a child!"

Robin, eyes squinted against the light, pushed back until his head bumped the wall. He wanted to scurry through the doorway before anyone caught him but the runner was almost upon him now. The spotlight created a glow around him and there was a hole in his left leg, mid-thigh. A chunk of his right hand seemed to be missing.

The runner fell to his knees in front of Robin, his momentum pushing him forward until their faces were inches from one another. Robin looked into the strangers wild eyes, smelt a terrible meaty smell and felt his head go light.

"Stay there," shouted a voice, hidden by the beam of the searchlight.

The runner turned, facing the shouter and got up.

"I said stay there."

The runner glanced back at Robin and took a step towards the chicken coop, then another, angling himself away from the boy.

The first shot tore off the top of his skull and four more bullets found his body before it hit the ground.

Robin closed his eyes and began to cry.

Two

The Bedford 3 Ton QL truck squealed to a halt at the unmarked crossroads. It was early morning, the sun having just crested the horizon and the windscreen was tinted with rich orange colour. Apart from the idling engine and the birds singing in the trees, everything was quiet. Sergeant Harold Lloyd, in the passenger seat, turned and hit the flat of his palm on the back of cab.

"Squad three!" he called, his voice echoing in the confined space. "Out now."

He nodded at his driver, got out and stalked to the back of the truck. Squad three had assembled at the tailgate, the corporal corralling his men who were busy shaking the stiffness out of their legs and rubbing the backs of their thighs.

"Ten-hut," said the Sergeant and the men quickly fell into line. "Corporal?"

The corporal stepped forward. Sergeant Lloyd checked the clipboard he'd held under his arm. "Corporal Ward, you and your squad are now part of Exercise Potter. You are to make your way to the town of Happisburgh, any way you choose, without being spotted by the police, army or Home Guard. They will be around, trying to find you. If you are found, you have failed the exercise and I will not be happy with you. Do you understand?"

"Yes, sarnt," said the corporal.

"These are your co-ordinates for the final target." He read the co-ordinates from his clipboard. The soldier nodded without writing anything down. "You won't hear them again and failure to arrive at the designated final post will result in you failing the exercise. Do you understand?"

"Yes, sarnt."

"You will be picked up at the designated point tomorrow morning at oh-eight-hundred hours. Go."

"Yes, sarnt," said the corporal and he nodded at his men. "Let's move out, lads."

Sergeant Harold Lloyd took a measured step backwards, watched the squad move away then marched briskly to the cab and got back in.

"Move along, driver," he barked and the Bedford pulled away.

Corporal Ray Ward watched the truck drive away, three squads still sitting in the back, then looked at his own men. His lance corporal, Joe Kelly, stepped up next to him and turned to their squad.

"Right, fall in you lot, first things first, let's get off this fucking road."

The men fell into line as Ray surveyed the area. Across the road was an orchard, the trees widely spaced and heavy with fruit. The easterly road, coming off the crossroads, cut between it and, a hundred yards down, there was a gateway. "Down there," said Ray, pointing, "it'll get us out of sight."

"You heard the corporal," said Joe, "let's move it."

The squad fell into step and marched down the road, the noise of their packs and weapons scaring a flock of crows that took flight from the trees. The gate was old and bent, secured to its post with old rope and beyond it was a concrete yard and the remains of a stone-built barn. Ray climbed over the gate and the others followed him into the trees. The light was muted, the angle of the sun not enough to cut through the foliage and in the first clearing, Ray shouldered his pack to the ground and rested his rifle against it.

"At ease, boys," said Joe and waited until they'd taken off their packs before moving to Ray's left side. "Fall in."

Ray surveyed his squad. He'd only met them last week, at the start of training at Thetford camp and, like most of the other corporals, had thought at first it was a joke. Fresh off the trucks, the men were given a number and told to stand in the PT yard and over the next couple of hours, as more trucks rolled in, more soldiers gathered until there were five men in each group.

For reasons that weren't explained, the exercise would consist of five-man squads, smaller than the normal minimum of eight. Each squad would be led by a corporal, assisted by a lance corporal.

It had been a hard week, for many reasons, but Ray felt quite confident with his men, though Joe Kelly was his secret weapon - perhaps ten years his senior, he had a lot of experience and an authority that made the men listen. Ray liked him and they seemed to have a mutual respect.

Arthur 'Gracie' Fields was the designated navigator. Tall and thin, with Groucho Marx glasses and sandy hair, he was good-humoured but quiet. He knew his way around a map and had found the way out of a dense wood for the squad in one of the Thetford exercises - by such a margin that the other squads were sent back in to do it again.

Alan 'Porky' James was balding prematurely though he appeared to be barely into his twenties and so only a few years younger than Ray. Stocky, taciturn and as hard as nails, he was the radio operator and carried the unit on his back, the antennae waving over his head. It took Ray a day or so to realise he was called 'Porky' because he came from Melton Mowbray.

The last member of the squad was Danny Price, known as 'Half'. Tall and handsome, he had the look of Clark Gable and made full use of the resemblance. It was alleged, during mess break one day, that if Half was posted somewhere for more than a day, he'd find a girlfriend there. Quick witted and sharp, he was adept at getting things for less than market value, a good skill for the squad.

"Okay boys," Ray said, "this is the situation. We've had a week of training, a week of getting to know each other and I think we're going to work together well. I don't know any more about the exercise than you do, but I do know I don't want us to get caught and sent back to Thetford for spud bashing."

A murmur of agreement.

"What time do you have Joe?"

The lance corporal looked at his watch. "Oh-eight-fourteen."

Ray checked and nodded. "Check your watches men," he said and waited until they had done so. "First things first, we need to find out where we are."

"We're east of Thetford," said Half.

"How far?" asked Joe.

"We left barracks at oh-seven-hundred," said Ray.

"We got here about oh-eight-hundred," said Half, "so call it an hour."

"But we had three drop offs before us," said Gracie, "about five minutes each time."

"Good point," said Joe. "If we assume an average of 40 miles an hour, that gives us forty miles, less the fifteen minutes for the drop-off. I reckon about 30 miles, give or take."

Ray looked at Gracie. "Give us a rough idea," he said.

Gracie pulled a large, folded map from his pocket, knelt down and spread it on the ground. Half and Porky knelt on either side of it, holding it down and Ray walked around so he could see the details.

Gracie put his compass on the map. "We maintained an east-northeast route for the most part, so thirty miles would put us east of Norwich, though we could be as far south as Loddon and as far north as Wroxham, depending on the angle." He pointed to both places on the map and people nodded their assent.

"Did you hear the co-ordinates from Sergeant Lloyd?" asked Ray.

"Yes corp," said Gracie and checked the gridlines. "Happisburgh's a little place right on the coast."

"Anybody heard of it before?" asked Joe but nobody had.

"What's the distance between us, assuming we're the southern end of where you estimated?"

"If we're near Loddon, we're looking at about thirty miles."

Ray turned to Joe, who bit his lip as he worked it out in his head. "Pick-up's at oh-six-hundred tomorrow, so we've got twenty two hours to do thirty miles."

"We need to sleep though," said Ray, "just in case they hit us with another exercise tomorrow."

"Okay, five hours sleep gives us seventeen hours to do thirty miles. Piece of piss."

"It doesn't seem so bad," agreed Ray. "They'll probably have plenty of patrols out, trying to spot us."

"No doubt," said Joe, "meaning it's thirty miles across country."

"Which is going to take longer," said Gracie.

"Fine," said Ray and stepped back to face the squad. "We know what we're doing, let's have a piss stop and then get moving."

As the men moved into the treeline to empty their bladders, Joe held Ray back. "Have you ever been on one of these exercises before?"

"No. Have you?"

Joe nodded grimly. "Couple of times, once in the middle of Wales where we got picked up easily by an MP squad and they beat the tar out of us."

"What?"

"It probably won't happen, but we need to be careful, of them and landowners. They don't always take kindly to people traipsing across their fields, even if it's in the National interest. Same Welsh trip, we had a shotgun levelled at us."

"Well, I hadn't planned to use this but just so as you know, if Farmer Palmer points his gun at us." Ray opened his pack and pulled out a .38 Webley revolver. "It might make him back off."

"Nice," said Joe.

"I picked it up off a dead officer at Dunkirk. It did me proud then and I'm more than happy with it now."

"Fine by me," said Joe.

They went to pee and by the time they got back, the men had pulled on their packs and rifles and were waiting.

"Plot us a course Gracie," said Ray.

Gracie checked his compass and at eight-thirty exactly, with Joe on point and Half bringing up the rear, the squad began to walk through the orchard, away from the road.

Three

The orchards were hard going, with uneven ground between the trees that threatened to twist ankles and low hanging branches that caught faces, backpacks and rifle barrels. As the sun rose, jackets stuck to sweaty skin and even though it was cooler in the dappled light, it was still hot work.

Soon, the orchards ended and they were left with the choice of open roads or wide, flat fields. Some were pasture, a mixture of sheep and cows, but most were arable and the wheat was high. Ray decided to cut through them, making the squad less immediately visible to anyone passing on the road, though their khaki uniform didn't exactly blend in.

At a little after midday they came across a small pond surrounded by a stand of thin trees and took a break, all of them gratefully slipping off their packs to sit on the hard-packed ground.

"Position, Gracie?" said Joe.

Gracie took out his map, unfolded it and checked his compass.

"We've been walking for about three and a half hours," said Ray, "so I'd give us ten miles."

"And we've kept a steady line," said Gracie, "so if we did start at Loddon, we should be here."

The squad crowded in to see where he was pointing. The map didn't give many clues, with large areas marked as dark green or blue. "I think we're heading into marshland," said Joe.

Ray nodded. "That might make it more difficult to keep off the road. What's the nearest settlement?"

"Could be two," said Gracie. "One's South Rainford, the other is Hansworth. Neither of them look particularly big."

"But towns mean people."

"And towns mean pubs too," said Half.

"We're not going for a pint," said Joe.

"It was worth a try," smiled Half.

"But," said Porky, "pubs could also mean MPs and soldiers. Somewhere to whet their whistles as they wait."

"Good point," said Gracie.

Ray looked at Joe. "What do you think, break here for a while?"

"Can't hurt, the sun's high and it's a bastard of a hot day. Let's have some grub, catch a bit of shade, move off in an hour. We've got time and if we go into the night, we won't have the heat."

When the squad set off again, the sun was past its peak.

"I'm sick and fed up of this wheat," said Porky, brushing his arms.

From the back, Half grumbled along with him. "It's alright for you lot, I get all your dust too."

The field they were walking through was bordered by a thick hedge. Joe was twenty yards ahead and held up his fist, stopping the squad. Ray carried on until he was standing next to his lance corporal. "What is it?"

"There's a road beyond the hedge and I can hear something coming."

"Heavy?"

"I don't think so."

"Light, like a motorbike?"

"Can't tell."

"Get everyone up here and behind the hedge."

Joe turned and signalled the others and they ran to catch up, keeping their heads low and gripping their rifles tightly.

"Under the hedge," Joe hissed as they ran by. He and Ray tucked in behind them, keeping pace and they all slid into the depression where the field dipped slightly before the hedge grew out.

It was an engine, that much was clear. Ray got to his knees and found a patch of hedge he could see through. A narrow country road lay beyond, with trees and hedges lining the opposite side.

"Here it comes," said Joe.

Ray tensed, ready to drop out of sight if it was an MP jeep or staff car. The engine sound grew louder and he realised he didn't recognise it. Closer still and there was a shape through the trees across the road, flashes of colour and the noise grew louder.

"It's a boat," he hissed. "On the other side of the road, there must be a river."

"There's water all over here," Gracie hissed back, "the map's full of it."

When the boat had passed, Ray stood up. "We'll make better time on the road," he said, "and it won't be so hard on our legs. The hedge runs close by, that'll give us cover if we need to move. If Joe could hear that boat as early as he did, we should be able to hear a jeep or bike."

Joe turned to the squad. "You heard the corporal, look lively."

The road was well maintained and fairly straight, bordered on the left by hedges and high, thick Oak and Ash trees. The water course was wide, the current slow and on the other bank, a line of trees gave way to pasture and meadows. The right side of the road was just hedges, giving them plenty of opportunity to dart through, should they need it.

They walked in silence, several yards apart from each other, Joe on point. Birds sang in the trees, unseen cattle lowed. An aeroplane went over at one point and they moved onto the verge, in case it was a spotter but it didn't even cross overhead.

After fifteen minutes, Joe held up his hand and stopped, waiting for Ray to catch up. "There's a building up ahead," he said. Ray could make out a stone wall through the trees but nothing else.

"We might have to go round."

"Transport," hissed Porky, who was bringing up the rear, "something's coming."

"Into the hedgerow boys," said Joe, his voice just loud enough to carry, "let's go."

Beyond the hedgerow was a narrow path bordered by tall reeds and Ray could see what appeared to be marsh beyond them. The path was wide enough for them to walk on and the hedge thick enough to hide them. All five got to their knees.

"Here they come," he said.

The heavy vehicle drove past at a low speed. "It's an Austin K5," said Half. When it had gone, he dropped flat on the ground and looked through the hedge.

"Loaded," he said, "there must have been twenty men in the back of that."

Ray and Joe looked at one another. "Are there any installations around here?" Ray asked.

Joe shook his head. "I don't think so, it must be part of the exercise."

"They were just regular troops," said Half, getting to his feet and brushing himself down.

"Armed?"

"Lee Enfields."

Ray pondered for a moment. "Well there's not much we can do, it could be something else entirely. We'll keep going but everyone keep an ear cocked."

Joe nodded. "Let's move it."

Gracie stood up and brushed himself down, stepping back as he did so. He bumped against Porky who said "Oi" and took a step backwards into the reeds. Even as Ray watched, Porky's centre of gravity shifted and a look of surprise crossed his face.

"Shit!" he called as he dropped out of sight, falling back into the reeds and grasping for purchase on them. There was a splash then he began gasping and coughing.

"Porky!" called Gracie.

Another gasp. "I'm okay," he said, coughing, "we must have been standing right on the bank, there's a little stream here."

"Get rid of these reeds," said Ray and grabbed a handful of the white stalks, twisting them and pulling back. With the four of them working together, a gap was cleared in moments and Ray could see the almost sheer bank, which dropped two feet into a muddy ribbon of water. Porky was standing up, water to his waist, a sheepish expression on his face.

"Sorry corp," he said.

Ray shook his head. "We didn't know. But we need to get you out."

Half and Gracie held out their arms. Porky waded to the bank, reached up and grabbed for them and they pulled him up onto the path. Water drained from his pack and clothes.

"The radio," said Joe.

"Fucking bollocks," said Porky and he shrugged it off, Gracie helping him to settle it. Even as they put it down, water puddled around the bottom of the pack. "I went in backwards," he said.

"How bad is it?" asked Ray.

Porky knelt down, switched it on. The unit made a strange noise but no lights were lit. He flicked the switch a couple of times and opened a panel. More water came out. "Fucking bollocks," he said again.

"It's fucked," said Joe.

"Shit." Ray took a deep breath. "How long will it take to dry out."

Porky looked up at the cloudless sky. "Well it's warm but, you know, we don't know how far the water got in. I'm really sorry corp."

"You didn't know," said Ray.

Porky got to his feet. "No, but…" His right boot caught the edge of the bank and, in his effort to not fall again, he threw out his arms and stepped backwards, almost falling onto Half. Half, his hands on Porky's side, staggered back a step.

There was a rasping sound, then a loud clang that was halted by both a meaty thud and Half's full-bloodied bellow.

Half fell back, his teeth gritted, tendons in his neck standing out like cords. "Fuck," he hissed, "fuck, fuck, fuck."

"What?" asked Joe, leaning forward, "what've you done?"

"My leg," Half hissed, "my fucking leg."

Ray looked down. Where Half had stepped back, his right foot was in the reeds. Joe knelt down and moved the reeds so he could see. He found the problem and looked up at Ray.

"What?" asked Half, "what is it?"

Joe pulled the reeds aside so they could all see. Fastened around Half's right ankle and biting deep into his lower leg was a man-trap. Made of black metal, the teeth had all but disappeared into the fabric of his trousers and blood was running through the holes they'd torn. Every time he moved or flexed his leg more blood ran out.

"Shit," said Gracie quietly.

Ray stared at the device. What the hell was a man-trap, that didn't look rusty or abandoned, doing in reeds by a stream in the middle of nowhere? Half hissed out a breath which snapped Ray back to reality.

"Let's get this off," he said. "Gracie, get the field dressings out. Porky, get out on the road, see if there are any more patrols coming. If you can't see anything, make your way south, there's a wall a few hundred yards up the road and there might be a house there. I don't care what you say, or what they say to you, we need medical attention immediately. Joe, you grab one side, I'll get the other."

"Corp," said Porky and he was through the hedge before Ray had a chance to kneel beside Half, who looked at him with a forlorn expression.

"Sorry corp," he said.

"Half, you didn't stand in it on purpose."

"The pack's ready," said Gracie, squatting beside Ray.

"Get the bandages," said Joe, "we're going to need to pack it and maybe put a tourniquet on too."

"Tourniquet?" gasped a panicked Half.

"Just in case," said Joe, patting the man's chest, "you're not going to lose your leg."

"I'm not?"

"You're not."

Joe looked at Ray and they locked eyes. He shook his head, raising his eyebrows. Ray shrugged. Neither of them knew what would happen.

Ray looked at Half. "This is probably going to hurt."

"Yeah," hissed Half. Gracie knelt beside his head and offered his hand. Half grabbed it.

"Do you know how to do this?" Joe asked Ray.

"Not at all."

"Okay, put your hands on the top bit," said Joe, spacing his hands so that he didn't touch the teeth and left enough room for Ray. Biting his lip, Ray touched the metal as gently as he could. Half's blood made it warm and slippery.

"One," said Joe. He looked at Ray.

"Two," said Ray and Joe nodded. They both pulled, the jaws of the trap opening slightly. Half let out an agonised cry and Gracie hissed out a breath as his hand was crushed.

"Pull," said Joe.

The two men tried to make purchase on the dusty ground but their boots were slipping and the metal teeth didn't want to part.

"It's not coming."

"Keep pulling," Joe gasped.

Both men were leaning away from the trap, Half tensed rigid, his hand crushing Gracie's.

"My hand's slipping," warned Ray.

"Keep pulling."

"I can't, it's…"

Ray lost his grip on the slick metal and it slammed back into place, blood surging through the holes in Half's trousers. He screamed and went limp and Gracie leaned over, checking the pulse in his neck.

"I think he's fainted, corp," he said.

"Probably for the best," said Joe. "Now he's out, let's get this damned thing off. Gracie, give us a hand."

"Wipe the blood off," said Ray, "it's impossible to get a grip otherwise."

Gracie did so quickly, mopping it with a bandage.

"Okay," said Joe, "we'll pull it as far as we can. Once it's clear enough that we can get his leg out, reach underneath Gracie and attach the clasp. That sets and disarms it, so it won't go on us again."

Gracie nodded. With the blood gone, Ray got a better grip and planted his feet, heels dug in. When Joe got to three, they both pulled and this time - though as hard as before - the move was smoother. Once the teeth were clear, Gracie reached under and clicked the clasp. Joe and Ray held Half's leg, one hand under his calf, the other cradling his heel as

Gracie pulled the trap down and away, throwing it aside. He took out fresh bandages as they laid Half's leg gingerly on the ground. The man groaned but didn't wake up.

"Joe, go after Porky and get us some help."

"Okay," said Joe and then he was gone.

"What shall I do?" asked Gracie.

Ray looked at the seeping holes in Half's trousers and realised he didn't know the answer. Stop the bleeding was obvious, but how? What damage had those metal teeth done? Could he make it worse, by doing something, or not?

Joe leaned through the hedge. "A Jeep's coming."

"Stay with him Gracie, I'll be back."

When Ray got through the hedge, Joe was standing in the middle of the road waving his arms over his head. The jeep was coming from the same direction as the Austin and as it got closer, he could see there were only two soldiers in it. They pulled to a halt thirty yards back and the passenger stood in his seat.

"Who're you?"

"Corporal Ray Ward, sir," he shouted. "We're on exercise and one of my men has stood on a man trap."

The passengers lips tightened into a line. "Is he badly hurt?"

"We don't know, there's a lot of blood and he's fainted."

The passenger conferred with the driver. "What unit are you?"

"I'm 3rd Rutlands," said Ray, "but we're on exercise."

Another quick conference. "We're heading to Sinclair House, they should be able to provide medical attention there. How many in your unit?"

"Four, with another further up the road."

"We'll pass him. Get your man out here."

"Yes sir," called Ray and cut back through the hedge with Joe. Trying to keep Half's leg as straight as possible, they managed to carry him through to the road. The jeep had moved up to the gap and the passenger, a sergeant, helped them put Half into the back. Gracie got in and sat with him, keeping pressure on the bandages and Ray and Joe perched on the side. The jeep took off steadily.

"What's Sinclair house, sir?" asked Ray.

The sergeant turned to look at him. "If Major Boothroyd wants you to know, he'll tell you."

Joe looked at Ray and raised his eyebrows.

"Sounds fair," said Ray and they made the rest of the journey in silence.

Four

Porky was half a mile up the road and the jeep pulled over to get him. As they drove into the grounds of Sinclair House, through gates manned by armed guards, it was obvious to Ray the site was being used for something important.

The house stood back a hundred yards from the gate. Once upon a time it must have been a country manor - there were a dozen windows on both floors, plus several more in the roof. Each windowsill was an exercise in fine stonework, gargoyles stood guard at downspouts and all three of the chimney breasts sported ornate, ironwork weather vanes. A dozen wide stone steps led to the double-breasted front door which looked like it was made of heavy oak.

To the left were stables, which had been converted to garages. To the right, beyond the sweep of the drive and edged with thick bushes, was a large lawn which gave way to an orchard. Underneath the trees, only barely visible from this angle, were several Nissen huts.

The jeep pulled to a halt outside the main door and two men in white smocks came out to greet it.

"What's happened here, Pearson?" the lead man asked the sergeant.

"I don't know, Dr Curtis, we picked them up on the way in."

"Excuse me, sir," said Ray, sliding off the back of the jeep and saluting. "We're on exercise and one of my men stood in a man trap by the reeds."

"Man trap?" repeated Dr Curtis slowly.

"Yes sir. We managed to pull it off but he passed out."

"I'm not surprised," said Dr Curtis and turned to his colleague. "Get stretcher bearers and prepare the theatre."

"You have a medical theatre here?"

Curtis looked askance. "Of course, doesn't everyone?"

Before Ray could reply, two stretcher bearers came through the front door, unloaded Half and, with Gracie running beside them, went back into the house.

Seargeant Pearson got out of the jeep. "Stay here, you three, I'll see if I can find Major Boothroyd."

"What is this place?" asked Porky.

"Who knows," said Ray, "and I doubt they'll be telling us too much."

"Could this be part of our exercise, Ray?" asked Joe.

"I wouldn't have thought so."

Sergeant Pearson re-appeared at the front door and pointed at Ray. "Follow me," he said, "you two stay there."

Ray marched up the stone steps and Pearson stood to one side to allow him through the door. The hallway had been converted into a reception area and in front of the wide staircase, standing off to one side, was a large desk. A woman of indeterminate age sat behind it, her hair as steely grey as her expression and she glared at Ray. Pearson cleared his throat and led him along a quiet, wood panelled corridor that seemed to stretch to the end of the building. Old portraits of long-gone people, some on horseback, stared down from the walls and they passed several doors, none of which were open but most had name plaques on. Midway down, Pearson stopped. He knocked on a door, waited until the person inside said "Come" and then opened it for Ray, letting him through. Pearson followed and closed the door behind him.

The office was large and airy, a big window across from Ray letting in a lot of light. The wood panelling was lighter than the corridor and there was only one portrait, of a horsebacked man about to charge into war. A leather sofa was against the wall to his right and two leather chairs were set in front of the large desk that dominated the room.

The man behind the desk had thick grey hair slicked back off a face round enough that lines didn't really show on it. His uniform was crisp and several medals were pinned to his chest.

Ray saluted.

The man behind the desk returned the salute, then peeled off his wire rimmed spectacles and put his hands together on the blotter. "Yes?"

"Corporal Ray Ward, I was brought here when one of my unit stepped into a man trap."

The man behind the desk stood up. He was barrel chested and shorter than Ray had expected. "Ah yes, the man trap in the marshes. Unfortunate circumstance, yes?"

"Yes," agreed Ray.

"My name is Major Desmond Boothroyd, I run the operation here. We have excellent medical facilities and your man will be well treated."

"Thank you sir."

"Are you on exercise?"

"Yes sir, from Thetford."

"An overnighter?"

"Yes sir, without detection."

Major Boothroyd smiled, as if they were now conspirators in some grand deception. "Shall we not discuss this, then?"

"We may have to, sir, if Private Price doesn't come back with us."

"As I understand it, the trap closed over his leg so he won't be going anywhere in a hurry. How far are you from your rendezvous point?"

"To be honest, sir, we were dropped blind and I'm not entirely sure where we are."

The Major laughed at that. "Ha! Well, my boy, if there's a bright centre of operations in this country, you're at the point it's furthest from and that would be about three miles east of Potter Heigham."

"Thank you sir."

"You and your squad are welcome to spend the night whilst Private Price is seen to by the medical staff and we can drop you at the rendezvous point in the morning. If your CO says anything, I will deal with him."

Ray nodded. "Thank you, that's extremely kind of you."

"Of course, only too happy to help. We don't get a lot of visitors here."

"Is it purely a medical facility?"

Major Boothroyd frowned. "I don't follow."

"This house, the operation. Is it a medical facility?"

"Not at all," said Major Boothroyd with a tight smile. "We are a rehabilitation unit, dealing with the poor souls suffering with post-concussional syndrome, or what used to be called shell-shock.

Our Dr Curtis has made some marvellous leaps forward with the use of electricity and we're already seeing progress with some of the PCS victims that have been assigned to our care." Major Boothroyd put his glasses back on. "Now, if that's all, Sergeant Pearson will show you and your men to your billet. Feel free to look around outside, dinner will be at eighteen-hundred hours precisely and you are, of course, invited to dine with us."

"Thank you," said Ray and saluted. Sergeant Pearson opened the door and they both marched out.

"Get your men, corporal and I'll show you to your billet." They marched back along the corridor, their boots squeaking on the tiled floor. "I can't provide you with a guide, but the layout of the place is straightforward and everything is signed. In the orchard, keep away from the Nissen huts as the Shockers can get agitated."

"Shockers, sergeant?"

"Our shell-shocked comrades-in-arms."

"How many of them are there?"

"More than enough," said the Sergeant and Ray looked at him. "Three of the huts are full, the fourth is about halfway. I don't know what's happening, corporal, but we seem to be getting more of these sad bastards every week."

"But Dr Curtis is developing treatment to help them."

Pearson looked at Ray. "If strapping wires to your head and running a dose of electricity through your brain is helpful, then that's good."

"You don't agree?"

"I didn't say that, corporal," Pearson said, his tone sharp.

Sergeant Pearson stopped in the reception area. "Gather your men. You're billeted in room 203, on the second floor. The infirmary, where your private is being looked after, is on the same floor at the other end of the building. The mess hall is down the corridor there." Pearson pointed to a corridor that opened to the left of the staircase. "Eighteen-hundred-hours sharp."

"Yes sir."

"Fall out, corporal."

Ray saluted and turned to the main door as Sergeant Pearson marched away towards the mess hall.

Joe, Gracie and Porky were beside the jeep, looking over the lawns towards the orchard and when Ray opened the door all three stood to attention.

"At ease," said Ray, trotting down the steps to join them. "How's Half, Gracie?"

"They wouldn't say, but he seems to be in good hands. Lots of nice nurses about."

"So what is this place?" asked Joe.

"Apparently it's a rehabilitation place for shell-shock victims."

"Poor bastards," muttered Porky. "My uncle had that, from the Great War. It was awful, like he was a coiled spring just waiting for something to set him off."

"Well apparently the doctor who's looking after Half has made some kind of innovation with electricity that's helping them."

"Helping them?" asked Porky. "Zapping people with electricity doesn't sound like a good idea to me."

"Or me," agreed Gracie.

"So what else were you told?" asked Joe.

"We're spending the night here, then they'll drop us at the rendezvous tomorrow and if we get any static from the CO, Major Boothroyd will vouch for us."

Joe nodded, his lips pursed. "A comfy room?"

"I don't know, we're in 203 on the second floor."

"I'll take our kit up," said Gracie.

"I'll come up with you," said Porky, "I need to get the radio dried out."

When Gracie and Porky had gone, Joe said, "How about a walk in the orchard? I wouldn't mind seeing what's in those huts."

"The Shockers, Pearson called them. Those must be their dorms."

Joe nodded. "So why do they need guards in the orchard? That's just odd."

"Pearson said to avoid going near the huts, Joe."

"I'll bet he did. But isn't it strange that this place has a platoon attachment? There're two guards on the gate, the drivers, the guards on the huts. For a rehabilition unit, that's a lot of men."

"Maybe because it's experimental?"

"Could be," said Joe. "Shall we walk?"

They crossed the drive, onto the lawn and Ray looked toward the chicken run. "Look at those birds," he said, "I'd love an egg sandwich."

"Maybe we'll get one at dinner," said Joe.

The lawn was overgrown and a natural walkway had been formed, the thinning grass leading them in a slow curve that edged them away from the house. Ray looked into some of the big windows and saw clerks, secretaries and then Major Boothroyd, who was still working at his desk. Ahead, the orchard ran from the perimeter wall on this side, along the back of the house and to the wall on the far side. He couldn't see the back of it, the denseness of the trees blocking his view.

The Nissen huts were laid out two a breast, the two at the back slightly off-centre so that parts of all four were visible. They were identical, with whitewashed brick fronts and corrugated steel roofs. The nearest was labelled 'Building 1' and had two windows, both barred and an inset front door. A light was fixed above the alcove.

"We'd better keep back," said Ray, "Pearson said the Shockers get agitated."

"It can't hurt to take a quick look though, can it?"

"Joe…"

As they got closer to Building 1, they heard moaning.

"What the hell is that?" asked Ray.

"It's coming from inside."

With each step, the moaning got louder. Joe was three steps away from the nearest window when a soldier appeared at the far edge of the building and pointed his Sten gun. "What're you doing, soldier?"

Joe held up his hands. "Nothing, I was just going to look in the window."

The soldier nodded his head sharply towards the hut. "Can't you hear them, you're making them antsy and we don't want that. Now turn around, lance corporal," he pronounced the rank as if the words had a bad taste, "and walk away."

"Yes," said Joe, not taking his eyes from the Sten gun. He joined Ray and the soldier watched them until they were walking alongside the back of the house.

"I told you," said Ray.

"But there's something strange there," said Joe.

"What do you mean?"

Joe shook his head. "I don't know, I can't put my finger on it, but something's crook."

Five

Room 203 was halfway down the long, wood panelled and white-tiled corridor that ran from the stair case to the far wing of the house. It had been converted into a ten-man dorm, with five sets of bunk beds against the left wall, ten lockers and a small sink on the right. A large window looked out over the orchard. Marshland stretched away beyond the perimeter wall, stopping at high sand dunes that hid whatever was behind them.

Porky was sitting on the bottom bunk by the window. He'd stripped some of the radio down, the parts lying on the windowsill to catch some of the afternoon sun. Gracie sat on the upper bunk two beds along, reading a letter. They both looked up as Ray and Joe entered the room.

"See anything exciting?" asked Gracie.

"Not really," said Ray, "just the huts, the orchard and an armed guard."

"An armed guard in the orchard?" asked Porky without looking up. "Those scrumpers must be persistent."

"He was very keen to keep me away from a Nissen hut," said Joe, "apparently the Shockers get agitated when people are around?"

"Shockers?" asked Porky, his attention caught.

"Their name for shell-shock victims." Joe sat on the nearest bunk and rubbed his face hard with his hands. "Heard a lot of moaning," he said.

"From the poor bastards?" asked Gracie.

"We think so," said Ray. "I'm going to check on Half, don't go anywhere."

The infirmary, according to the signs at the staircase, was at the other end of the house and Ray walked along the corridor, which had been painted a calming white. He was alone but could hear someone calling out and another, softer voice trying to calm them. All the doors he passed were shut and none had plaques on them.

The infirmary took up the whole wing. Offices on both sides of the corridor had been knocked back and a large set of double-doors filled the corridor. A desk was set up in front of them, the nurse behind it writing something in a folder, facing Ray. She wore a grey ward dress with a scarlet-trimmed cape and a white pinafore with a large red cross over her chest. Her hair was bunched up into a starched white linen head-dress. She smiled at Ray as he approached.

"Can I help you?"

"I'm Corporal Ray Ward, you have one of my men in your care, a Private Daniel Price."

The nurse closed the folder she'd been writing in and picked up another, opened it and ran her finger down a list. "Ah yes, leg wounds. Do you want to see him?"

Ray nodded.

"Through here, along the corridor and he's in ward 3."

"Thank you," said Ray and he pushed through the doors.

After the relative brightness of the corridor, it took his eyes a moment to adjust to the gloom of the infirmary. He was in a narrow corridor, the walls and floor painted a pale green, the doors on either side all closed, viewing windows shuttered to cut out any natural light. The ceiling had been lowered and although there were several large light fittings, none of them were on. The doors were numbered one to ten and as he passed, he could hear movement and moaning from inside them, then someone called out like before. He heard the softer, gentler tones of the nurse who was trying to calm her patient.

The claustrophobic corridor opened into a wide, bright space that seemed full of windows. Wards had been built on either side but the area was well lit and stretched at least one hundred yards to the end of the building.

Matron sat at the nurses station to his left, checking a chart. Somewhere in her thirties, with dark hair pulled up into her hat, she had a thin face that might look friendly if she smiled.

"Good afternoon, corporal," she said, looking up and offering the tightest of smiles. "I take it you're here to see Private Price?"

"If that's possible."

"You're in luck, come with me please." She led him to ward 3, which looked out over the front of the house. It housed four beds, two of them occupied, a sleeping man in the one nearest the door. Half was across the room next to the window, sitting up reading a newspaper. A box, under the covers, protected his leg. He smiled as Ray entered.

"I'll leave you to it," said Matron, "but please be considerate of Mr Freeman who's sleeping."

"Of course," said Ray and he sat on the hard wooden chair beside Half's bed. He glanced out of the window and watched a guard move from behind one of the Nissen huts.

"Afternoon, corp," said Half.

"How are you?"

"Feeling good, all things considered."

"You had us worried there, I didn't expect you to be in a ward yet."

"The doctor says I'll be okay, the teeth didn't catch anything they weren't supposed to. They took me straight in, stitched me up and told me not to play any footy for a while."

"We're staying overnight and the Major is going to arrange us transport to the rendezvous tomorrow morning."

"So am I coming back to your billet?"

"I would think they'll keep you in here until the move."

"Yes," smiled Half, "very good, corp."

His tone made Ray smile. "Which one do you have your eye on?"

"A pretty little blonde thing, she was in here a while back. I told her I might be a bit grubby, you know, from rolling around in the dirt and should probably have a bed bath."

"And what did she say?"

"She suggested I ask Matron."

They both laughed and the sound was loud in the confined space, making Mr Freeman snuffle in his sleep and turn over. Matron appeared at the door and glared at them.

"I'll leave you to it, Half, please don't get into any more trouble."

"I won't, don't worry."

With a nod, Ray left him and stopped in the doorway, in front of Matron.

"Corporal, I did say…"

"I apologise, Matron, it wasn't intentional."

"Well, Mr Freeman needs his sleep."

"And he'll get it, Private Price wasn't being noisy."

Matron nodded and as they stepped into the main area, the patient from the closed room off the corridor moaned loudly. They both looked in the direction of the sound.

"Poor bugger," said Ray, "it sounds like he's in a bad way."

"It affects people in different ways." Matron's tone had changed, softened. "They can't help it, it's not their fault. It makes me so mad, this assumption that a lot of it is cowardice. Did you know, in the Great War, there were nineteen British military hospitals that were solely - solely, mind you - devoted to the treatment of PCS. Even ten years after, there were still sixty-five thousand veterans receiving treatment. You look at those poor souls and…" She paused, touched her left hand gently to her chest. "Well, there but for the grace of God go I," she said.

"So how does the treatment work?"

Matron looked as if he'd asked her age. "That's Dr Curtis' department, we look after the cases as they're brought in, to try and get them to a stage where they can go down to the huts."

"And how do you do that?"

"We assess each patient and try to settle their surroundings, by explaining where they are and who we are and making them understand they're safe. Bathing is good, as are massages but the key is a complete rest of mind and body. Mr Freeman, who you almost woke up, was one of our more vocal cases but we've worked well with him."

The person moaned again, louder this time until the soothing tones of the nurse settled him.

"When were you born, corporal?"

"Nineteen twenty-one, ma'am."

"So you might not have experience of this. Would you like to see one of our patients?"

"If that wouldn't be a burden."

"Of course not, I think it's important to understand. Follow me."

Matron led Ray into the narrow corridor and stopped at room four. Ray could hear movement from behind the door but nothing vocal. Matron reached for the viewing window and twisted a knob that opened the blinds.

"This is Mr Metcalfe, we welcomed him last week from Africa."

Ray peered in.

The room was bare, except for a bed pushed up against the wall in the far left corner and a large window let in plenty of light. Mr Metcalfe, who showed no signs of having heard the blinds being opened, was staggering in circles in front of the window wearing only underpants, his arms swinging by his side and occasionally straight out, as if to aid his balance. As he walked, his right leg stiff and unbending, he held his body at an unnatural angle, as if he was trying to twist his trunk around. After another circle he stood still, tottered slightly and fell, breaking his fall with his arms. His legs continued to move, shifting his body when his feet caught the floor and his head rolled on his neck. After a moment or two, he lay still, staring at the ceiling, before kicking his legs to get himself into a sitting position. He struggled to stand up, gripping tightly to the bedstead but the effort was just too much and he fell again. Then, with a sudden spring, he lurched up and ran towards the window where he grabbed the frame as if trying to stay on his feet.

"Jesus," said Ray.

"Indeed," said Matron.

"I'm sorry, but that's appalling."

"And Mr Metcalfe isn't one of the worst."

From behind them, the moaner began again but this time his voice rose until he was screaming. The nurse, her soothing tones not working, raised her voice too. There was a clatter and Matron turned. Another clatter and she quickly crossed the narrow corridor, Ray right behind her.

"Nurse Minton? Nurse Minton, is everything okay?"

There was a muffled sound that didn't make any sense.

Matron turned towards the main area and called "Situation!" Within moments, three nurses were rushing towards them and there was another clatter from inside the room.

"Nurse Minton?" called Matron again and when there was no response, she turned to her colleagues. "I need the kit before we can go in, go and get it."

Two of the nurses ran off.

"Is there anything I can do?" asked Ray.

Matron turned, as if she'd forgotten he was there. "Yes, you can leave corporal, we need the room."

Something hit the door hard and Matron opened the blind, gasping as a man's face appeared to fill the window. Ray had never seen anyone with the mans shattered expression apart from, perhaps, in nightmares.

"I need that kit!" shouted Matron.

At the sound of her voice, the man looked at her but it was clear from his thousand-yard-stare that he didn't see anything. Three large bruises littered his forehead and where the hair was shaved at his temples, the skin was blackened as if it'd been burned. His wide open bloodshot eyes were tinged with yellow and a deep wound, oozing blood, sliced his left cheekbone.

He pushed back and Ray saw that the nurse was wearing the padded clothes of a dog trainer. Her thick outfit prevented her from bending her arms properly to fend off the attack of the patient and he leapt onto her, forcing her down and out of sight. There was another scream.

"Get that kit here now" yelled Matron. She turned, saw Ray standing transfixed. He couldn't drag his gaze away from the awful sight, the accumulation of despair that this narrow corridor contained. "Corporal, I told you to leave."

"Yes ma'am," he said and took a step away as the other nurses came rushing back. They were carrying a padded jacket, a large bag, a big glass syringe and what looked like a billy club. As Matron pulled the jacket over her uniform, Ray pushed through the double doors and the smiling nurse in the corridor welcomed him.

Six

The mess hall was formed from three of the dorm-sized rooms knocked together, the canteen section at the far end with several long tables set out in front of it.

There were probably fifteen soldiers in the room, mostly sitting by the windows and at least half as many nurses. Two Matrons sat together on their own, Major Boothroyd shared a table with Dr Curtis and several NCOs had co-opted another table. There was a lot of conversation, most of it low-key.

When they had their food, Ray led his squad to a table near the main door and Gracie looked round as they sat down. "A lot of people," he said.

"It's a big house," said Porky.

"I know, but…"

Ray thought back to what Joe had said as they walked to the orchard but didn't say anything.

"It's military," Porky continued, "they're working with shell shock victims. There might be something going on here that they don't want getting out."

"Like what, Porky?"

The radio operator looked at Joe. "I don't know, corp said there was something about electricity."

All three of them looked at Ray. He'd told them everything, when he returned from the infirmary and they'd listened without saying much until he got to the madman.

"Those black marks," said Joe, "could they have been burns?"

"I suppose so."

"Electrical burns," said Porky, nodding. "I've had that a couple of times, taken a handful of electricity by mistake and the tips of me fingers were black for a few days."

"So they zap electricity through people's heads?" asked Gracie.

"Apparently so," said Ray. "It's supposed to be getting good results."

"And does it?"

"I don't know. But if I was the first man I saw, whatever they could do to straighten me out would be much appreciated." He looked from Joe, to Grace, to Porky. "I've never seen anything like it I honestly haven't. Even watching the old newsreels didn't affect me like this. It was awful, the poor soul was just trapped in that body."

"If that was me," said Joe, "I'd want them to try zapping me."

"And me," said Porky.

"I'm not saying I wouldn't," said Gracie, "but…"

"But nothing," said Porky. "If it's a choice between spending the rest of your days spinning around an empty room like a top or getting to go home and see your girl and your family and start again, what would you do?"

"When you put it like that," Gracie nodded, "I'd say yes."

"Of course you would," said Porky and began to eat his dinner.

"It still doesn't explain all the soldiers though," said Joe quietly.

"So what do you think?" asked Ray.

Joe shook his head, speared some potatoes. "I don't know, but there's something about those Nissen huts that bothers me."

"You said that before, what do you mean?"

"I don't know, just a feeling. All these huts, a secured area, armed guards, it doesn't stack up. I just want to see who's in them." He bit his lip. "Do you think it'd be worth trying again?"

"To go and see them?" asked Gracie.

"We wouldn't get near, the guard was on us straight away before, wasn't he?" said Ray.

"I know, but it must be a different soldier down there now, perhaps he might be off having a crafty snout or something."

"Well let's try it again then," said Ray.

The mess hall began to empty by eighteen-thirty-hours.

"Shall we?" Ray said and they made their way back up to their billet. At the top of the stairs, Ray glanced out of the window at the front of the building and saw several soldiers, their Sten guns drawn, running towards the orchard.

"What's going on?" asked Joe.

Somebody shouted and a car engine started.

"It could be anything," said Ray, then paused as they heard more shouting.

"Should we go and see?" asked Joe.

"You know, I think that might be a good idea."

"What about us?" asked Gracie.

"Go along to the infirmary and try to get in to make sure Half is okay. Porky, the radio should be dried out now, see if you can get anything on it."

"Corp," the men said together and split up. Ray and Joe started down the stairs. At the reception, the desk now empty, they heard heavy footsteps and four soldiers ran from the direction of the mess hall and out through the front door. Ray and Joe followed them, across the drive and onto the lawn. The chickens were squawking now, flapping their wings and bashing into one another.

There was more shouting from the direction of the Nissen huts as they got close to the edge of the house and then Major Boothroyd strode around the corner and saw them instantly.

"Attention, corporal!" he called. Ray and Joe stopped running and snapped to attention. "What are you pair doing out here?"

"We heard the commotion sir," said Ray, "we thought we might be able to offer some help."

"And you know what the commotion is?"

"No sir."

"No clue at all?"

Reluctantly, Ray said, "No sir."

"The situation will be under control in a few minutes," said Major Boothroyd. "Thank you for your concern, but we won't be needing your assistance. Go back to your billet, get a good nights sleep and be ready to ship out at oh-six-hundred tomorrow."

"Yes sir."

There was still shouting and Ray wanted to loiter to find out what it was but the Major was glaring at him. He saluted, turned and marched away with Joe at his side.

"Shit," said Joe, when they reached the gravel, "we were so close."

Sergeant Pearson came out of the house, talking loudly to his corporal. "How did the hell did it happen again?"

"They're getting smarter, sir," said his corporal.

Sergeant Pearson passed Ray, almost looking through him and then they were gone. Ray and Joe looked at each other.

"What the hell is going on?" asked Joe.

Gracie hadn't been able to get in to see Half, the nurse on the desk refused him entry point blank and when he tried to charm her, Matron appeared in the windows of the main door and shooed him away.

Porky had managed to dry out the remainder of his parts and was busy reconstructing the radio.

Nobody knew what was happening.

Joe broke out a pack of cards.

Seven

Shouting woke Ray up. As he reached for his watch, Joe said, "It's just after three, Ray."

"What is it?" Ray asked, rubbing his face.

"It woke me up a moment or two ago, sounds like it's out in the orchard again."

"Have the others woken up?"

"I don't think so."

"Shall we go and have a look?"

"I was wondering if you'd ask."

Both men dressed quickly and Joe checked the window, pulling the heavy drape to one side. "Nothing out here," he reported.

Ray opened the billet door and found the corridor quiet and dark. They crept along to the staircase, sticking close to the wall and making sure they didn't bump any of the doors. Ray pulled one of the drapes aside at the window. Light was seeping into the sky, though it was still dark and he could see two guards at the gate but no other movement.

"Clear out there," he said.

"Shall we go downstairs?" asked Joe.

"Might give us some trouble with the Major," said Ray, "but I'm curious now."

Joe started down the wide stairs, Ray close behind. They'd descended three risers when there was a muffled yell and a crash from behind them. The sound was startling and Ray felt an immediate rush of adrenaline.

"The infirmary," he said and they rushed back up the stairs and along the corridor. The nurses station was empty. The windows in the double-doors were covered by blinds though the one on the right had been knocked and light shone around it.

There was another shout from inside the infirmary, muted this time, followed by a door slamming.

"We have to go in," said Ray. "Are you ready?" He took a deep breath, suddenly aware of how hard his heart was pounding and pushed the doors.

"Shit," said Joe.

"Oh my God," said Ray, pushing the door wide, "what the hell…?"

"This is hell," said Joe.

The lights in the main area were on but here, in the narrow corridor, almost all the fixtures had been smashed and one of those remaining was blinking on and off. The floor was littered with glass and bloodied footprints and something at the far end that looked like a dark rag. Two of the doors were hanging off their hinges and two others had their windows smashed.

"What the hell happened here?" asked Joe.

"I don't know. Half's ward is through there."

"Lead on, corp."

Ray pulled his pistol from his pocket, tensing and relaxing his fingers on the grip. "Take the left side and follow behind."

At the first doorway, he crouched low and looked around the jamb. The room was empty, the bed on its side. Two bloodied hand prints were on the wall under the window.

"All clear," he hissed and watched Joe edge towards the first door on his side. He peeked around the frame and looked at Ray. "Clear."

Ray shifted to the next doorway but that room was clear too, as was the next. He paused before the next doorway, the room the bloodied man had been in before. He felt a cold sweat line his upper lip and tested his grip on the pistol again as he remembered Matron putting on the thick padded jacket.

The room was empty.

He breathed a sigh of relief and nodded at Joe, who moved forward and checked the next room cautiously but it was also empty. He reached forward, to flick away the dark rag and threw himself backwards, gagging.

"What is it?" hissed Ray.

"It's not a rag," Joe said and groaned.

"What do you mean?"

"I think it's part of someone's scalp," Joe said, getting to his knees.

"What?" Ray edged across the corridor and could see, even from a couple of feet away, that Joe was right. The piece of scalp was the size of a fist and the long black hair attached to it was matted with blood.

Something clattered and there were pounding footsteps. Ray looked up as a nurse came rushing out of one of the wards towards them, her hat missing, her hair pulled loose. There were bloody handprints on her pinafore.

"Help!" she yelled.

"Over here!" called Joe and Ray aimed his pistol beyond her.

"Don't let him get me," the nurse shouted, "please."

Somebody was standing in the ward doorway, wearing only his hospital pyjama top. His legs were dirty, his knees raw. He held onto the door frame as if trying to get his balance.

Ray looked at the man, trying to take everything in at once and felt a chill run through him. There was blood across the mans lower face and splashes that extended up across his forehead. His closely shaved head was blood spattered too and a large wound had been gouged on top of his skull. A black burn mark was weeping pus above his left ear.

The nurse saw the scalp, pressed her hands to her mouth and tried to change direction but slid in some of the blood, falling heavily to one side. Joe grabbed her ankles and pulled her behind him, then tucked behind Ray.

"Stay there," Ray called to the man who looked at him blankly. "Joe, is she okay?" He risked a glance behind him. The nurse was sitting up, her knees to her chest, taking deep breaths. "Are you okay, love?"

"No," she said, staring at the scalp.

"What the hell happened?" asked Joe.

"They're getting smarter," she said, her breath hitching.

Joe looked up. "That's what Sergeant Pearson said."

Ray nodded, not taking his eyes off the nurse. "What's your name?"

"Fiona." She hitched in another breath that almost threatened to become a sob. "Fiona Kilpatrick."

"What do you mean about them getting smarter, Fiona?"

"The Shockers," she said.

There was a low moan and Ray snapped his attention back to the man who'd now moved out of the doorway into the main area.

"Stay there," he shouted, "or I will shoot."

The man opened his mouth and Ray realised there was hair caught in his teeth. He blinked, swallowed back bile. "Was it him?" Ray asked over his shoulder. "Did he bite off someone's scalp?"

Fiona nodded, began to cry. "It's a skeleton crew on the night shift, I hate doing it. We had a couple of problem cases, I don't know how Mr Mulligan got his door open but he did. Sally didn't stand a chance."

An alarm began to sound, loud in the narrow corridor, startling them. There were raised voices but they sounded far away. Ray glanced at the main door, expecting someone to come through but nothing happened. How could people not hear this?

He turned back. "Are you Mulligan?" The man tilted his head, as if trying to understand a foreign tongue.

"Yes," said Fiona, "but he won't understand you and couldn't tell you even if he did. He was one of the first, he bit his tongue off during the electro-shock-therapy."

Mulligan began to shamble towards them, one arm on the wall to keep his balance, the other hanging at his side.

"Stay where you are," Ray shouted. Why weren't there soldiers coming through the door to back them up, surely other people had heard the commotion?

"We didn't know how far we could go," said Fiona, almost to herself. "Dr Curtis just said it was trial and error. The first man, it was horrible, his head caught on fire. I still hear his screams when I close my eyes. Mr Mulligan was after that, but still not right. We use tongue-clamps now."

Mulligan was coming closer. "I will shoot you," shouted Ray, "stand down, soldier."

"He won't stop," said Fiona, as Mulligan took another step.

Ray bit his lip, wishing there was another way but realised he didn't have a choice. He swallowed, his dry throat clicking. He'd never shot anyone before but Mulligan was still coming towards them. Please stop, he thought. But it was no use. Trying to keep his aim steady, he aimed for Mulligan's left arm and fired. The noise, in the claustrophobic space, was hugely loud and Fiona yelped.

The bullet was on target, ripping a hole in Mulligan's sleeve and knocking his arm from the wall. He went down in a heap, staring towards Ray, moaning unintelligibly. Then he started to get up.

"Stay on the floor!" called Ray.

"He won't," shrieked Fiona, "don't you see? He's already dead."

"Already dead?" said Joe.

"He didn't survive the treatment but Dr Curtis figured out how to reanimate him. That's what this is, that's what this whole set-up is about."

Ray glanced back at her. "Bollocks, what about the shell-shock victims?"

"That's what they come here as," insisted Fiona.

There was a burst of automatic gunfire from outside in the grounds. Ray glanced towards the windows and then at Mulligan, who was shambling towards them again. "Stand still!"

"You need…" started Fiona, but then stopped.

"What?" asked Joe, "he needs to what? Fiona, he's getting closer."

"Oh my God!" she shouted, staring at the ceiling as if imploring them to understand her. "You need to shoot him in the head, that's the only thing that'll stop him."

It was insane, completely insane. Ray looked at Mulligan, took in his blank stare and the blood stains on his top. "Joe?"

"Ray…"

A bead of sweat ran down Ray's left temple. He tried to hold the gun steady, aiming it at Mulligan's leg but his hand was shaking. If he shot the knee out, that'd take the man down.

"Shoot him!" shouted Fiona.

Mulligan kept coming. "I can't," Ray said finally, "I can't shoot him in the head." He took careful aim and pulled the trigger, the pistol bucking as the flash seared into his retina. A bloody hole appeared in Mulligan's left kneecap and the man went down as his leg gave way.

"His head!" Fiona shouted, "his head!"

Ray turned to her. "I couldn't. Joe, let's get her out of here, we'll regroup with the others."

"Yes sir," said Joe, quickly getting to his feet and pulling Fiona up, his hands in her armpits.

"He's not down," said Fiona, pointing.

Mulligan was getting to his feet, pushing himself up the wall with his good leg.

"I don't believe it," Ray said.

With a shriek, the thin-faced Matron came rushing out of Half's ward and caught Mulligan in a rugby tackle with enough force to put them both on the floor. They slid until a table stopped their momentum and then she was straddling him. The right side of her face was bloody and long red streaks coated her pinafore and dress.

"You bastard," she screamed, hitting him in the face, "you bastard!"

Mulligan made no effort to protect himself. Matron concentrated her punches around his eyes until one of his cheekbones sank. Even as she hit his eye sockets with the flat of her palm, Mulligan didn't move.

"Glenda!" yelled Fiona and Matron looked up. She was missing a hank of hair from just above her right ear.

"Get out of here Fiona and take them with you." She glared at Ray. "You shouldn't be here, Corporal Ward."

"No," Fiona said and shrugged Joe off, rushing to her colleague.

"Yes, you know what's happening…"

Mulligan reached for Fiona, shifting sideways and catching Glenda off balance. She fell onto her side and Mulligan grabbed for Fiona, pushing himself along with his good foot. Glenda, clearly exhausted, got shakily to her feet and took several deep breaths, blood running freely down her face.

"Go, Fiona," she yelled, staring at the table top and the scatter of things that had been knocked over on it. She picked up a porcelain bed pan and straddled Mulligan again. He turned, as if vaguely aware he was being restricted but made no move to push her off.

Raising her hands high, Glenda brought them down fast, the pan caving in Mulligan's right temple. She hit him again and again, until his forehead was a bloody mass and a fresh fine spray of scarlet was painted up her uniform. Fiona, her arms around Glenda's shoulder, had a bloody mist across her face.

"Leave it, Glenda," she said, "come on, we can go."

"He bit me, you stupid cow, look at my head. He bit me."

"We can sort it out, come on."

Glenda got up quickly, startling Fiona and grabbed her by her shoulders. "He bit me, that means I'm going to turn. Get out of here."

"I won't leave you."

"Then I'll brain you with this as well," Glenda threatened and lifted the pan above her head.

"No, come on…"

Glenda shoved Fiona away. "Corporal Ward, shoot me."

"What?" It didn't make sense. "I can't shoot you."

"Corporal, shoot me now, in the head. That's an order."

"I'm not going to shoot you, Matron."

Glenda hit herself in the face with the pan hard, breaking her nose which spread across her face. A gout of blood caught Fiona in the eyes and made her gasp.

"Holy shit," said Joe.

Glenda hit herself again, the force of the blow knocking her backwards. Her feet tangled in Mulligan's arms and she went down, hitting the edge of the table with the base of her skull. To Ray, it looked as if she was dead before she hit the floor and blood bloomed around her head.

The three of them were motionless for a moment and then Fiona took a deep breath and screamed.

"Joe," said Ray, snapping out of it, "grab her and shut her up in case there's anything else in here. I'll get Half."

Trying to avoid the blood and pointing his pistol ahead, Ray ran to Half's ward. The lights were off but it was plain to see all the beds were empty. Half's was made, with no paraphernalia around it.

"What the hell?" He turned a complete circle, wondering if he'd made a mistake and come into the wrong ward. He rushed back out to the open area. Fiona was bent over, leaning against the wall, a pool of vomit between her feet. Joe was rubbing her back and looked up as Ray came through the doorway.

"Where is he?" asked Joe.

"There's nobody in there, I'll check the next one."

The next ward was also empty. Ray ran back to Fiona. "Where is he, where's Private Price?"

"He was taken downstairs after mess."

"What do you mean?"

"What I say. The Major sent a couple of soldiers up, they took him down to Dr Curtis."

Ray and Joe exchanged a look. "What does that mean?" Joe asked. He looked from Mulligan to Glenda. "And why hasn't anyone been up here to find out what the hell is going on?"

"I thought the same thing," muttered Ray, "but it's not quiet outside either. I'll look after her, you get Gracie and Porky and meet me at the staircase."

"Okay," said Joe, sounding pleased to be doing something. Avoiding the blood on the floor, he ran down the narrow corridor and out the main doors. As they opened, Ray heard more gunfire.

Ray grabbed Fiona's arm. "Do you need to get anything before we go?"

She looked at him, her eyes wide and red, her cheeks slick with tears and streaked blood. "No. Please don't leave me."

"I won't, my lance corporal has gone to get the rest of my squad and we'll meet them in the corridor. I need to find my soldier though, I need to find Private Price."

"I understand, I'll help, just don't leave me alone, please."

Ray held her hand and she gripped his tightly as he led her down the narrow corridor. As they passed the scalp, Fiona looked at it and shivered. "You should have shot him in the head," she said.

"Yes," said Ray, "I think you're right."

Eight

The others were already at the staircase landing by the time Ray led Fiona there. The commotion from outside was much louder here, even over the alarms, with lots of shouting and gunfire. Ray checked out the window but couldn't see what was happening though the dawn was spreading pale orange fingers across the sky.

The squad was ready. Gracie faced back towards the billet, his rifle raised. Porky, radio strapped to his back, pointed his rifle down the stairs. Joe held his rifle at his side as he slid off Ray's pack and handed it to him.

"Are you okay?" he asked Fiona.

Fiona nodded slowly, wiping the blood and tears from her face with a handkerchief.

"We need to find Half," said Ray. "Fiona says he was taken downstairs while we were in the mess hall."

"That's why they wouldn't let me in," said Gracie.

"Maybe. Has Joe briefed you about what happened in the infirmary?"

"Too fucking right," said Porky. "If anyone other than you two had said it, I wouldn't have believed it."

"I wish it wasn't real, I really do."

"Do you think all the people in those huts are zombies?" asked Gracie.

"Who knows," said Ray, "I'm not even sure what a bloody zombie is."

"I saw a zombie picture at the flicks once," said Porky, his voice as calm as if they were in a pub discussing it. "It had Bela Lugosi in it."

"Nice," said Joe, "tell us about it later."

"We'll go downstairs," said Ray, "and see if Half is down there. If not, we'll try and find the Major or Sergeant Pearson or the doctor. Somebody must know where he is. Then we're getting out of here."

Joe tapped Gracie on the shoulder and motioned him towards the stairs. "Porky, take point, then the Corp and Fiona. I'll bring up the rear with Gracie."

"Do we shoot?" asked Porky.

They all looked at Ray. "Yes," he said, "warn them once then shoot the bastards in the head."

As they went downstairs, the sounds of shouting and gunfire from outside were louder. Ray could hear people running and barking orders.

At the reception, Porky checked right and left before beckoning everyone else on.

"The Major's office is along that corridor," Ray said, pointing. "Most of the doors have name-plates, so we'll go along and find him. Porky, stay here with Fiona and keep out of sight."

"If we go behind the stairs, I can still have a good view."

"Smart thinking, Porky, do that."

Fiona grabbed Ray's arm. "I want to get out of here," she said.

"I know and we will, I promise, we just have to find our friend."

Nodding to Porky, they moved off to the darkened corridor that only had three lights for the length of it - one near to them, one midway down and the other at the far end, which flickered as if the bulb was about the blow.

"Let's not waste time, boys, especially with that battle going on out there. I'll take the offices to the front. Joe, you take the back ones and Gracie, you sweep along behind us. Let's find Half and get out of here."

"And be careful," said Joe.

Ray nodded and tried the handle of the first, unmarked door. It was locked, as were the next two. Joe's were open and he dropped behind, checking them with Gracie standing back. Ray kept moving, keen to find Half.

He saw movement from the corner of his eye and pressed his back against the wood panel as he turned. A partly open door was across the corridor. Had it moved, or always been like that? There was no sensation of movement now. He glanced back at Joe and Gracie, who were edging towards him. The portraits on the wall between them seemed to glare down into the corridor, as if angered by the soldiers' presence.

Ray pointed towards the open door and Joe stuck up his thumb, moving along until he was only a few yards away. Using hand signals, Gracie moved to the other side of the doorway and Joe, crouching, pushed the bottom of the door with his rifle. It swung open onto darkness.

Gracie put his back to the wall and edged to the door. "On three," he said and reached around the frame, his hand patting the wall. It seemed to take a long time before the light in the room clicked on.

Even though it was a low-wattage bulb, they could see the office was empty. A desk was against the back wall, the black-out drapes covering the windows. Two filing cabinets stood guard and a single wooden chair showed them its back.

"All clear," said Joe.

The plaque on the next door read 'Dr Moore'. When Ray tried it, the lock unlatched. Crouching, he pushed it open gently and the heavy smell of blood carried on the air. Quickly, he reached for the Bakelite switch and, blinking against the glare, flicked on the light.

It was another office, the same as the one they'd just seen except this also had a narrow treatment table under the windows. Ray stood up and walked into the room. The man in the chair was wearing a white coat but Ray didn't know if this was Dr Moore or someone else and he wouldn't be able to ask the question either. The man was slumped across the desk, his service revolver in his right hand. He was facing the window, the entry bullet wound against his right temple. There was a lot of blood pooling on the blotter.

"Jesus," said Ray and went back to the corridor. Joe and Gracie had moved further on and he wanted to call them back, to tell them what he'd found but didn't. What good would it do?

The next door bore the plaque 'Dr Ironside' and was locked. From up ahead there was a loud bang. Joe glanced back and Ray nodded. They ran down the corridor, trying to judge which room the sound had come from, Ray looking at the plaques.

"Major Boothroyd," he said.

The door across the corridor clicked and moved slightly, making Gracie jump. "Shit," he said.

"We'll take that," said Joe, "you check the Major, Ray."

Nodding, Ray put his ear to the door but heard nothing. Gripping his pistol tightly, he pushed the door handle and it clicked open. There was a scuffle of movement and Ray crouched down. The gunshot was a poor aim, the bullet thudding into the wood somewhere above him. Ray got on one knee, his pistol forward and aimed at the desk where the Major was standing, staring at him.

"Put down the gun, sir," said Ray.

The Major looked at his revolver, then at Ray, then at a space over the door. "I could have shot you, you bloody idiot."

"There's a lot of that going on, sir."

"What are you doing here?"

"I'm looking for my soldier who went into the infirmary."

"Well have you tried up there?"

"Yes. And saw a man who was dead having a fight with a Matron who'd had a chunk of her scalp bitten off. But no Private Price."

Major Boothroyd took a deep breath, looked at his revolver and put it on the blotter, then sat heavily in his chair. "It's all turned to shit, corporal."

Ray stood, lowering his pistol and glanced behind him. Joe was standing by the open door on the other side of the corridor and Gracie came out of the room, shaking his head.

"Where is he, sir?"

Major Boothroyd traced the pattern on the handle of his gun with his finger. "Who?"

"Private Price. He's gone."

Major Boothroyd looked up, an annoyed expression on his face. "Is he all you're worried about? For Christ's sake man, can you hear it out there? Everything's gone to hell and you're concerned about one man."

"This is your concern sir, I just need my man."

"I applaud your tenacity, corporal, but I'm afraid it's too late."

It took a moment for the full impact of his words to hit Ray and when they did, he raised his pistol again. "What do you mean, what have you done with him?"

Major Boothroyd waved away the threat of the gun. "He was fodder, don't you see? You all were, placed in our lap like a gift from the gods."

"Fodder?"

"Yes," said Major Boothroyd dismissively, "what else would you be?"

Ray felt anger burn in the pit of his belly as he stared at the Major, not quite believing what he was hearing. "Soldiers, for King and country." He glared. "Sir."

"And now in our project. Nobody would have missed you and your little squad, corporal and we had a need for you."

Ray took a step towards the desk. "Tell me where Price is or so help me god I will shoot you in the face.

To Ray's astonishment, Major Boothroyd smiled. "That or let them get me, I know which I'd prefer."

"Let who get you?"

Major Boothroyd exploded, slamming his hands on the desktop and pushing himself to his feet. "This war isn't just about you, you know, we have to fight and come up with new weapons, we have to take care of our soldiers."

"By what, frying them with electricity?"

"Dr Curtis is a good man, was a good man. He had an idea to help the poor shell-shocked bastards but nobody knew, at first, what would happen if the treatment went on too long. He was as startled as the rest of us with what he discovered but well, what a weapon."

"Weapon?"

"The walking wounded, you fool. We set out to try and save the shell-shocked, with the best of intentions and along the way discovered that our treatment, if pushed too far, could militarise their bodies. We could have a battalion of the undead, three-hundred or fifteen-hundred men at a time, marching into war and impervious to damage, to fear, to climate. Hitler and his forces wouldn't stand a chance."

"You're mad."

"Am I?" Something bashed against the window and the Major flinched. "And now, they have come to reap what we have sown."

"What's happening out there?"

"My men are being over-run, I should imagine. It can only be a matter of time."

"Ray!" shouted Joe from the corridor. "Come here!"

Ray stepped to the doorway as an ashen-faced Joe met him there. "He's here."

Taking a last look at Major Boothroyd, Ray followed Joe across the corridor. Gracie was kneeling in the doorway, a puddle of vomit in front of him.

Ray looked through the door and, at first, thought the three bodies were standing on their own two feet until he saw the leather harnesses they all wore. Suspended from the ceiling, each person was clearly dead. The one furthest away was short - Ray thought, at first glance, that it might be a schoolboy - and only had half of his right leg, which appeared to have been amputated none too cleanly above the knee. His torso was riddled with bite marks, his left hand was missing and a large gouge had been torn from his throat. Half was the middle body, his face coated with thick blood. The tooth marks from the man trap had been opened somehow so they gaped, the red flesh too bright against the paleness of his leg. There was a large wound on his right side at the waist and it took Ray a moment to realise that somehow his body had been torn. A loop of intestine had popped out and was slowly sliding down his leg. A man in hospital pyjamas, his back to Ray, was tugging at Half's right leg, as if he wanted to complete the separation so he could run off with a bit of him.

"Hey," Ray called and the man turned. He had the same blank stare as Mulligan had.

"Shit," said Gracie.

The gunshot was sudden, loud and welcome. A black blossom flowered in the man's forehead and he fell backward, his arm looping in Half's intestine and pulling more of it out. Ray looked at Joe and the smoking rifle.

"I had to do it, Ray. Fucking Shockers."

"I know."

Two more men in pyjamas moved from the back of the room, towards them. Another couple were in the shadows on the other side of the room.

"I count four," said Joe.

"Me too. Gracie?"

"Four," he said and Ray heard movement behind him. "No," he screamed, "five…"

Ray turned. Gracie was on the floor, his hair being tugged by a Shocker whose head had been shaved badly, the burn marks above his ears glistening. Gracie was struggling to get back to his feet but didn't have the leverage. Ray took a couple of steps back and raised his pistol as two more men appeared in the doorway. One lurched towards Ray, taking him by surprise and knocking him off balance. The other fell onto Gracie.

"Corp, he's biting my fingers, get him off me."

Ray tried to shrug the man off. Joe came to help but, with no clear shot, had to shoulder his rifle to free his hands. He grabbed the attacker as Gracie screamed.

"Help him!" Ray shouted.

"We will, I need to help you first."

Ray wrapped his hands around his attackers neck, pushing up to open a space between their chests. Joe slid his rifle across the man's sternum and pushed up, knocking him off Ray. Ray got instantly to his feet.

"Corp!" screamed Gracie. His left hand was now fingerless and the two Shockers were biting chunks from his neck and chest.

Ray heard the rifle discharge three times. Gracie held out his right hand. "Help me, corp!"

"He's bitten," said Joe.

"I know." Ray took a deep breath, raised his pistol and shot Gracie in the forehead. The Shockers continued to feast.

"There's one left."

"I shot Gracie, Joe. They were eating him."

"You did the only thing you could, Ray."

"I fucking shot him."

"And now you've got to shoot them."

Ray looked at Gracie, his body jerking as the two men pulled at it. He lifted the pistol, shot one just behind the ear and put his gun to the base of the others neck before pulling the trigger. He kicked both bodies off Gracie.

Joe fired his rifle again. "We're clear, sir."

Ray took in the carnage of the room. "What hell is this?" he asked. "Let's get Porky and Fiona and get out of here."

With a last glance to their fallen comrades, they went into the corridor. As they passed Major Boothroyd's office, he was sitting at the desk with his head in his hands. People were hammering on the window and it sounded like it wouldn't be long before they smashed it.

"I found Private Price," Ray said and the Major looked up. "He was in that room over there. What was it, some kind of training thing?"

The Major didn't say anything. The window smashed behind him and he jumped in his seat. Hands pushed through, knocking the drape aside and letting in the pale rays of early morning sunshine.

Ray closed the door.

Nine

The reception area was clear and Ray called for Porky as he ran into it.

"Corp?"

"Yes, you can come out."

Fiona led the way from behind the staircase and Porky smiled when he saw Ray and Joe. Then he looked around. "Where's…?"

"Half was already gone, Gracie bought it down there."

"Bugger."

Ray grabbed his shoulder. "We did everything we could, Porky."

Porky looked at him, his eyes shining and nodded.

"Joe," said Ray, "we need a plan."

"We don't know what's going on outside."

"Let's assume it's bad." Ray turned to Fiona. "Any ideas?"

She looked at him and bit her lip. "There are garages on the right as you go out, they're usually full of jeeps and trucks but I don't know how many there'll be."

"Is there any way in or out other than the front gate?" asked Joe.

She looked from Joe to Ray. "I don't think so."

"We can't make a decision until we know the situation outside."

"We can't really open the door, Ray," said Joe.

"If we go into one of the front offices, couldn't we look out the window?" asked Fiona.

Ray clicked his fingers and pointed at her. "Yes. Lead the way."

"But I don't…"

Ray smiled at her. "Go on, lead the way."

She tried to smile at him and almost succeeded. "That one would be good," she said.

Joe went to try the door she'd suggested. "It's locked."

Without warning, Porky strode across the corridor, lifted his leg and pistoned it against the door handle. Wood splintered and he kicked it twice more until the door opened fast enough to bang off the wall.

"We're in, corp."

Fiona rushed to the window and crouched, waiting for the others. Joe stood to one side and gently pulled the blackout drape up from the windowsill.

It was lighter outside, the sky a pale grey. Two make-shift gun emplacements had been set up with sandbags in the drive and a handful of soldiers were lying on the grass, their guns aimed towards the orchard. Littered around them were dead bodies, most with gunshot wounds though a few had bloody holes in their uniforms. Those corpses had been shot in the head. Nobody was shooting at the moment but several people were shouting.

"If we go out the front door," said Joe, "how far are the garages and can we get in there without anyone seeing?"

"They're not far," said Fiona, "probably the distance from this window back to the staircase."

Ray turned and made a quick estimate. "Fifty yards?"

"But we'll be spotted by the troops in the drive and whoever is heading towards those machine-gun-nests," said Porky.

There was the vaguest hint of movement to the far left and the soldiers on the grass began firing. The emplacements didn't, sitting patiently until the gunfire had finished.

"That's when we go," said Ray, "when they start firing."

There was no more sound from the other end of the corridor, though Ray kept looking back at that awful office, expecting one of the Shockers to come lurching out, blood smeared around his mouth. He kept seeing Half, hung up and almost broken in two and then Gracie, screaming for help - God, those images would stay with him forever.

The front doors were open a crack and they squatted next to them, listening. Orders were being shouted, threats were made and although Ray didn't know what had happened, from what he could hear, neither did anyone else.

"How do we play this, corp?" asked Porky.

"Quickly. A good pace will get us to the garages in no time. Joe takes point, I'll bring up the rear and unless someone gets in your way, keep going."

"What if someone does get in our way?"asked Fiona.

"Then go through them," said Ray, "do whatever you need to do. We didn't ask to be here, we didn't ask to be in the middle of this, we're getting out."

"I don't have anything," she said, holding her hands out, palms up.

"Can you use a rifle?" Joe asked.

"I've had some training, but it's been a while."

"Hang on," he said and ran down the corridor. Ray looked through the gap in the door. A sergeant was walking between the gun emplacements, talking to the soldiers, his words lost on a breeze.

At the sound of footsteps they all turned as Joe came back, holding a rifle.

"It was Gracie's," he said as he handed it to Fiona, "I'm sure he'd have wanted you to have it."

"Thank you," she said and cocked it.

There was a shout. Ray saw the sergeant running towards the main gates. As he got close, a dozen or more Shockers came through the hedges, grabbing for him. The sergeant tried to stop and turn at the same time but his momentum carried him forward even as he was falling backwards. He landed hard, his head bouncing off the gravel and the Shockers were on him. The soldiers in the emplacements turned their guns towards him but more soldiers ran to the drive from the lawn, blocking their shot.

"Now's our chance," said Ray, "let's go."

He pushed open the door and let Joe go past him, gave Porky a shove and Fiona followed close behind him. Ray went out behind her. Outside, the skirmish had commenced and the sounds echoed against the house, gunfire punctuated by screams that made Ray's blood run cold. Two dead soldiers, their foreheads broken and bleeding, lay at the bottom of the steps, their Sten guns beside them. Ray stuck his pistol in his pocket, grabbed the two guns and ran to catch up with his squad. Joe was already at the door of the first garage, pulling at the lock but it wouldn't move. He took a step back, fired at the surrounding wood three times and kicked the door. It gave and he was in, pulling Porky and Fiona through. Ray checked the main gates, which were now crowded with soldiers and Shockers, then slipped through the gap and Joe pulled the door shut.

"The main gate's blocked," said Ray and looked around the garage. Brick-built, the floor was concrete and clean. Cans of oil and a couple of tool boxes were on the work benches across the way and behind him were several ladders. The back wall was bricked and there was a single pedestrian door, the glass panel in it covered with a white X. There were no vehicles.

"Wrong bloody garage," muttered Joe.

Ray handed him one of the Sten guns. A stray bullet hit the door at the far end.

"So what now corp?" asked Porky.

"It'll be too risky to try and move to the next garage but staying in here isn't going to help us."

"What about the river?" asked Fiona

"Swim?" asked Porky, "I'm carrying a bloody big radio, you know."

Fiona glared at him. "Of course not, silly, there're boats."

"Where, moored up here?" asked Joe.

"I don't know," said Fiona and her voice cracked. "I don't know, I didn't pay that much attention, oh why is this happening?"

"Hey," said Joe, grabbing her shoulders, "look at me. Look. At. Me." He waited until she did. "You've got us out here, you've held your nerve and you've kept up so don't crack on us now."

She shook her head, then offered him a half-smile. "Piss off, soldier," she said.

Joe smiled, a big grin that lit up his face. "That's my girl."

Ray walked to the pedestrian door, Porky behind him. "Cover me," he said and tried the handle. It wasn't locked. He glanced back at Joe and Fiona. If he opened the door and a horde of Shockers were out there, they were rightly caught between the devil and the deep blue sea - Shockers in front, Shockers in back. He gripped the Sten tighter - he might be able to stop a few before they were over-run. "Don't forget, go for the head."

"I've got you, corp," urged Porky, as if to say 'let's go'.

"Yeah," he said and opened the door, dropping to a crouch with the Sten gun pointing up. There was nobody outside, just the most tranquil view he'd seen in a long time. The sun was now up, the sky tinged navy and orange. Trees swayed gently in a breeze and the river moved at a steady pace. He could hear birds singing, the gurgle of the water, the annoyed honk of a goose.

"Down there," said Porky, stepping into the doorway as Ray straightened up. A flight of wooden steps led to a landing jetty some twenty feet below. There were three other flights of steps along from them, one for each garage. He could see four mooring posts, two of which had small craft tied to them, rowing boats and a couple of canoes. The mooring post below the garage next door had a larger craft, pointing the way they'd come from yesterday.

"What is that?" he asked.

"Bloody hell," said Porky, "that's a motor yacht. A thirty footer I'd have said."

"What?" asked Joe, crowding in for a look.

"They've got a bleeding yacht," said Porky happily. "We get on that, we're off."

"Can you drive a yacht?" asked Ray.

"Drive?" Porky looked at him, grinning widely. "Sail, corp. I might come from Melton, but my Dad loved the coast. We was out at Kings Lynn most summers and I used to hang around the beach and docks all the time. Some of them boat owners took pity on me, let me go out with them at times."

"So do you know how to sail?"

"Corp, if I can start the bleeder up, it's just a question of steering."

"Good enough," said Ray and led the way down the steps. Outside the garage, the sound of gunfire was much louder now.

On the jetty, Ray helped Fiona onto the boat as Porky shrugged the radio off and untied the mooring ropes. Joe grabbed the radio and jumped on board, then Porky got on at the stern. He knelt in front of the wheelhouse and, within a few moments, the engine coughed into life.

"Joe," called Ray, "stand by at the front, keep an eye out for anyone, we don't want any more sailors."

"What shall I do?" asked Fiona.

"You take the right side, I'll take the left, keep your eyes peeled."

"But it's just fields my side."

"If we start shooting at people my side," Ray said, " you can come over."

"Ready?" called Porky and Ray gave him a thumbs up. The engines surged and the boat pulled away from the jetty. "This isn't going to be fast, corp!"

"Just so long as it moves."

The garage door burst open and a Shocker came through, missed his step and careered over the handrail of the staircase. Ray watched him freefall and land badly on the jetty. It took the man a moment or two to get to his feet. His head lolled back, as if his neck was broken and bone poked through the bare flesh of his right leg. The Shocker took two paces before falling sideways into the river.

Another came through the door, slower this time. He remembered the soldier saying to Sergeant Pearson about them getting smarter and Ray wondered if it was true. This Shocker came down the stairs carefully as another appeared in the doorway.

"Porky, we could do with some more speed. Joe, company back here."

"I'm doing my best!" yelled Porky.

Joe worked his way down the boat. "Are we picking them off?"

"If we fire, I'm worried we'll draw interest."

"Agreed. If Porky can pick up the speed, we should be clear of the house in no time."

There was a splash as another Shocker went into the water. The first still hadn't surfaced but this one began to do a rudimentary front crawl.

"Oh my God," shouted Fiona, pointing, "it's coming after us!"

Another went into the water, then another. More appeared at the doorway. The boat was edging towards the corner of the perimeter wall now and Ray bit his lip, trying to decide what best to do - fire on the swimmers and risk alerting the soldiers to their presence, or do nothing and hope they didn't swim faster than the boat could move.

The first swimmer gave up, his face in the water as he floated towards the far bank. The second swimmer was still coming, but slowing. The third swimmer was just behind him.

"Nearly there," said Fiona, gripping Ray's arm. He looked up as the corner of the wall went by. The gates were still closed, the sound of gunfire and screams seemingly unreal, as if they were coming from a gramophone played a long way away.

"Keep it going, Porky," he said, "keep it going."

"There's a plane," said Joe, pointing away from the back of the boat, "a Lysander."

"Could it be a spotter, coming to see what's going on?"

"May be."

"We're passed!" said Fiona, a big smile on her face, "we're away."

Ray glanced over, saw the wall and gates a short distance behind them, then checked behind Joe. Another of the Shockers was floating face down, nudging the opposite bank.

"Porky," he said, "you're a genius, well done."

"Thanks, corp."

With a sudden movement that startled them all, a Shocker launched himself over the stern in a spray of dark river water. His fingers snared Joe's shoulder and the two of them fell to the floor in a tangle of arms and legs as they struggled. Porky grabbed the Shockers left ankle and tried to pull him away. Ray grabbed his right foot but the man's grip was complete. Joe, getting pulled along too, tried to prise the man's fingers loose and snapped some of the bones but the Shocker grabbed him with his other hand and Joe yelled out. Fiona rushed in, her rifle raised and brought the flat end of the stock down hard. The Shockers forehead collapsed and she ruptured his left eye socket but he kept hold. She hit him again, again and again, crushing his head and screaming as she did so until soon she was hitting pulp.

Porky and Ray let go of the Shockers legs and Ray reached for Fiona, holding her arm. She was crying.

"It's done," he said, "we're clear. Come on, Joe, up you get."

"Shit." Joe was staring at the blood running down his hand and the ragged stump where half his index finger had been bitten off. "Oh shit."

Ray looked at Joe, watched the blood drip onto the deck. He glanced at Porky who wouldn't meet his gaze and Fiona, who was looking at her feet.

Joe looked at them all. "Shit," he said.

Story Notes

This started with a Facebook message in late January 2015 from Adrian Chamberlin, inviting me to contribute to an anthology called *After The War* which he and Frank Duffy were editing for Terry Grimwood's Exaggerated Press. I readily agreed to contribute, though I'd never written anything set in a war before and began thinking through possible scenarios on my evening walk. I came up with the idea of some soldiers on exercise during World War 2, who find themselves trapped in a building and as the days (and walks) went on, I realised they were trapped by zombies but knew I didn't really want to have flesh-eaters all over the place. Around this time, I happened to see something online about shell-shock victims (Mr Metcalfe's actions are taken directly from a quite distressing clip I found on YouTube) and that was my link - what if an out-of-the-way place was experimenting on shell-shocked soldiers and inadvertently stumbled on the ability to re-animate the dead?

I took my basic idea down to Mum & Dad's one evening and we spent a lovely hour or so chucking around ideas, as I asked Dad plenty of technical questions (he's a real WW2 buff) but it was Mum who came up with the idea of the rushes and someone falling in the water.

In my original plan, the squad was dropped at Potter Heigham, Joe nipped out to the nearest town for clues and we'd have a POV of Half as the ghouls came to get him, but everything else was the same. I dropped some ideas - *"soldier falls into an almost empty silo with a zombie, has to shoot his way out"* and *"on the marshland, hiding in a puddle as zombies walk by"* - because they weren't necessary but the ending was set *"a zombie has strayed aboard and bites ONE. zombie is killed and thrown overboard. the survivors look at ONE's bite and have to decide what to do with him…"*

The characters took a while to gel in my head but, once they had, they fitted together well (and allowed for some nice little bits of comedy), with the friendship between Ray and Joe both surprising and pleasing enough it was tough to have him bitten at the end (even though it's the best emotive ending). I also decided, very early on, to write everything from Ray's POV - if he doesn't see or hear it, the reader doesn't see or hear it. The exception is the opening chapter, which I added after realising the first two chapters were character based and we didn't get any real action until the man trap.

I did a little research myself but Dad was a real hero, he pre-read the first three chapters (which are probably the most technical) and came up with some great suggestions to push things along. In addition, Kim Hoezli pointed out some logic holes, David Roberts gave me some good points about the infirmary sequence (the porcelain bed pan is his) and Sefton Disney is responsible for it being the Matron who is scalped. Just in case you thought it sounded familiar, Boothroyd's line "Well, my boy, if there's a bright centre to operations in this country, you're at the point it's furthest from and that would be about three miles east of Potter Heigham." is a paraphrase of Luke's comment in "Star Wars".

The anthology - a beautiful edition with a great Ben Baldwin cover - was launched as *Darker Battlefields* at Edge-Lit 5 in Derby, on July 16th 2016 (I wrote about it on my blog here - http://markwestwriter.blogspot.com/2016/07/edge-lit-5-derby-16th-july-2016.html) but, for whatever reason, didn't gain much traction. I've always thought that was a real shame, which led me on the path to re-publishing this.

I enjoyed the process of writing **The Exercise**, I think it's a zombie tale that is both very British and not really about zombies (though it's nicely gruesome at times) and it has some good set-pieces I'm particularly pleased with.

Acknowledgements

Thanks to Mum & Dad, for pretty much everything, as well as that evening discussing zombies in the Fens; Alison, for listening and reading and encouraging; Dude, who listened to the plot as we walked one afternoon and, with typical teenage candour, summed up the experience with "yeah, it's alright Dad…"; David Roberts (and Pippa), for the plotting walks; Kim Hoelzli, Sefton Disney and Chris Shepperd for the critiques; Nick Duncan; Sue Moorcroft; Stephen Bacon; Wayne Parkin; Adrian Chamberlin and Terry Grimwood (my original editor and publisher, respectively); The Crusty Exterior; Ian Whates and the NSFWG gang; The FCon and Edge-Lit crowd (who I miss dearly) and you, for taking a chance on this ebook.

Biography

Mark West lives in Northamptonshire with his wife
Alison and their son Matthew. Since discovering the
small press in 1998 he has published over eighty
short stories, two novels, a novelette, a chapbook,
two collections and six novellas (one of which,
Drive, was nominated for a British Fantasy Award).
He has more short stories forthcoming and is
currently working on a crime/thriller novel.

Away from writing, he enjoys reading, walking,
watching films and playing Dudeball with his son.

He can be contacted through his website at
www.markwest.org.uk and is also on Twitter as
@MarkEWest

The Exercise

The Exercise

Printed in Great Britain
by Amazon

59006902R00052